Contents

This book is dedicated to all the children who have entered my life through the doors of Walberta Park School. They have taught me so much.

I also want to thank . . .

. . . my extraordinary family and friends for their unyielding support.

. . . Jo-Ann Burns for her invaluable assistance throughout the writing of all Phoebe's™ adventures.

. . . Patricia Quinn and Kathleen Nadeau, for giving me the opportunity to tell my stories.

–B.R.

To brothers and best buddies Max and Ryan and my best brother Frank

–K.S.

Phoebe Flower's Adventures:

Phoebe's Tree House Secrets

by **Barbara Roberts**

illustrated by Kate Sternberg

ADVANTAGE BOOKS

Library of Congress Cataloging-in-Publication Data
Roberts, Barbara A., 1947-
    Phoebe's tree house secrets / by Barbara A. Roberts ;
    illustrated by Kate Sternberg.
        p. cm. —

ISBN 0-9714609-0-6

10 9 8 7 6 5 4 3 2 1
Printed in the U.S.A.

1
Fabulous Phoebe

After I read my *Most Thankful For* essay and announced to the class that Robbie Vaughn III was my best friend, the strangest thing happened. I thought for sure that, for the rest of my life, I would be as lonely as my purple hoola hoop that's been lying on the garage floor for three years. I thought as soon as the whole class found out Robbie was best friends with a girl he would get on his bike and ride as fast and as far away from me as he could. I was also sure Gloria and Elizabeth would tell everyone what a loser I was to have a boy as a best friend. Then, of course, there was Jooling, but she never talked to me anyway, so there I'd be . . . me, myself, and I, all alone.

So when Robbie high-fived me, I was shocked. He liked the essay and said it was the nicest thing anyone ever said about him.

Elizabeth grabbed my arm on the way out the door and said, "Great essay, Phoebe, Gloria definitely did not deserve to be your best friend."

Jooling looked at me and smiled.

Gloria wasn't even mad. She said, "Phoebe, you are so funny. What a trick you played on me!"

The best news was I got a big A+ on the paper. Mr. Blister told me he was very pleased at how well I wrote. My mom and dad were so proud of me. "See, Phoebe," Mom said, "let your heart do your talking and you will always do well." That night Mom made me my favorite dinner of meatloaf and baked potatoes. When you have a great day like that, you want it to last forever.

"Why, may I ask, are we having Phoebe's favorite dinner tonight?" Amanda, my big sister, asked. "What fabulous thing did she do?"

"Yuck, meloaf," Walter, my little brother said.

"Amanda and Walter, we are having meatloaf tonight because Phoebe got an A+ on her paper today and we are celebrating," Mom announced.

"I get A+ on all my papers," Amanda said, "so I think we should have liver and onion sandwiches every night. That's my favorite."

"Yucky, yucky, yucky, poo," said Walter.

"In fact, Mother and Miss Brain of the Year," Amanda announced, "I am entering a contest and everyone knows I will win because everyone also knows I am the best writer in my class. I have to write a five page paper on 'What Makes a Good Citizen.' It will be judged on both how neat it is and how well it is written. When I win, I will be going to Washington, DC, with my teacher. Then you can eat all the meatloaf you want. I'll be eating lobster with the president."

"Please try to be happy for Phoebe, Amanda. Thank you for understanding," Mom said and smiled.

"So what was this fabulous paper about, Phoebe, brainiac?" Amanda asked.

"Well, it wasn't really that big of a deal. I just wrote about my best friend," I told her.

"What did you say that was so special about Gloria?" Amanda asked.

"Well, it wasn't about Gloria," I answered.

"I don't understand this conversation," Amanda said. "Who could it be about, Phoebe? You don't have any friends. Personally, I could never understand why Gloria spent her time hanging around you."

"Phoebe does have friends, Amanda," my mom

said, "and her best friend is not Gloria, but Robbie. She wrote that in her essay, read it to the class, and got an A+."

"You have got to be kidding me!" Amanda stood up and screamed. "You didn't stand up in front of the class and say a boy was your best friend. I mean, Robbie's OK, but he's a boy. Are you crazy? How can we possibly be related?"

"Amanda Flower, one more word like that and you can go to your room. Do you understand?" Mom took her pointer finger and aimed it at Amanda's face.

"Yes, Mom," Amanda whispered.

When Mom turned her back, Amanda looked at me and mouthed, "You are such a loser, Phoebe."

I can't figure out why Amanda hates me so much. My mother told me that when I was little I sat on Amanda's lap for hours. She rocked and sang to me and read me books. Maybe she hates me for getting too big to sit on her lap. Some day I'll ask her, but certainly not tonight. Tonight, I'm afraid of what she might say.

Mom let Robbie come over and have ice cream sundaes with us. She said we could eat them in my tree house in the backyard.

"Hey, Phoebe, I've got an idea. Let's build some

4

walls in this old tree house and put some spy holes in the walls," Robbie suggested. "We can get binoculars, and spy on everyone in the neighborhood and no one will see us. We'll be able to see right into Amanda's room from here, too."

"That's a very good idea, Robbie. It can be just ours and no one will know where we are," I answered.

"It will be so great, Phoebe," Robbie laughed. "I can't believe we didn't think of it before. My dad has some old wood in the garage and I know where he keeps his hammer and stuff."

"My dad is coming here for Amanda's birthday and a meeting with Dr. Getset next week so he can help us, too. I know he will," I told Robbie.

"We can hang out here, eat snacks, listen to music, play cards, and do homework in peace and quiet," Robbie said.

"Well, I don't know about that, Robbie. Doing homework anywhere is not a fun idea for me. Plus, if I have to do some, I like to do it with loud blasting music," I told him. "It helps me concentrate."

"OK, OK, no homework," Robbie smiled.

2
I'll Be
the Teacher

Well, maybe no homework in the tree house, but I sure had a lot of it in the house-house. It seemed like I could never catch up. Mom was always checking on me, too. "Phoebe, did you do your homework? Phoebe, let me check your spelling. Phoebe, practice your math facts with me."

It seemed that Mr. Blister was only happy with me one or two days a week. I just couldn't seem to get all my homework done. Most days I couldn't even find the list of what I was supposed to do that night. I always wrote it down, but some days I'd forget to bring it home from school or it would fall under my seat on the bus or I'd use the list to wrap up my leftover lunch.

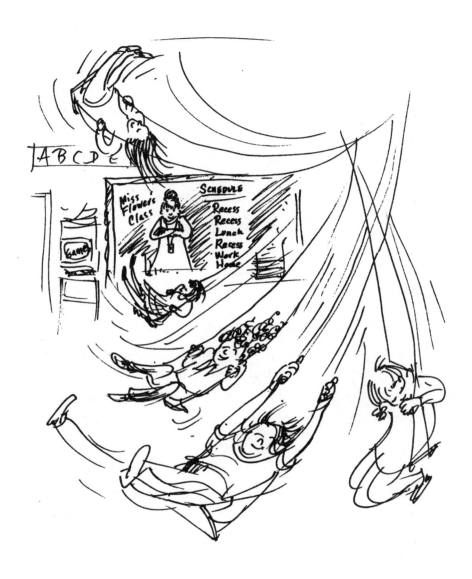

Everyone thought I was so cool for writing my A+ essay. That was good, except that I had a lot more friends. I began to learn that more friends meant more talking and more talking meant more trouble and more trouble meant more time in Dr. Nicely's office.

Last week in class, Elizabeth passed me a note about Gloria's socks. One was blue and the other was black. Gloria always, always looked perfect. Her dad even ironed her socks. Now that I think about it, it wasn't even that funny, but when I read the note, I laughed so hard through my nose that I snorted and everyone turned around to look at me, even Gloria. That made me laugh even harder.

I was still seeing Dr. Getset, the school psychologist, and we were becoming good friends. We would talk about school, my friends, my mom and sister and dad. I liked Dr. Getset because he made me feel that if he could pick anyone in the world to talk to, it would be me. What I didn't like about him was that when I told him Mr. Blister wasn't fair he said, "Now Phoebe, what would you do if you were the teacher?"

"Dr. Getset," I told him, "if I were the teacher, every kid in my class would have a swing instead of a desk. Before the kids in my classroom could go home they'd have to swing up and touch the ceiling with their toes. In my classroom, kids would have recess most of the day and work twenty minutes a day. If I were the teacher, Dr. Getset, when someone didn't do their homework, I'd take them to Disney World because that would mean that they needed to play more than the other kids."

He didn't like that answer, but he smiled anyway.

"Phoebe," Dr. Getset explained to me, "because you have ADD, it is harder for you to concentrate and stay focused. It's easier for you to play because it's OK to go from one thing to another thing when you play. If you're cleaning your room and you have to have it done before dinner, then going from one thing to another thing isn't OK because your room doesn't get cleaned and someone gets angry with you. The same thing happens with school work. Next week, when I meet with your dad and mom, we're going to talk about how you can stay focused on your school work so that Mr. Blister won't be angry with you."

"If you really believe Mr. Blister will stop getting mad at me, you probably also believe that someday it will rain orange soda, Dr. Getset."

"No, Phoebe, I believe it will be grape," he laughs. "Right now, Mr. Blister is trying some classroom changes. That's why he changed your seat to the front of the room and gave you a schedule to put on your desk. You know, the schedule you drew your tree house on?"

"Isn't that a great tree house, Dr. Getset?" I asked. "It doesn't really look like that exactly, but Robbie and I are going to work on it and when my dad comes to visit he is going to help us and we can spy on everyone and no one will know it."

"It does look like a beauty, Phoebe," Dr. Getset said.

I thought about what Dr. Getset said and I did notice Mr. Blister picked me to be the messenger more than any other kid. At first, I thought it was because he thought I was a good messenger, but now I think it's because he was trying to understand that I liked to move around a lot. I loved to get picked, so I'd go straight to the other classrooms and straight back.

Mr. Blister also put up a list of classroom rules on the blackboard behind his desk. He said, "Boys and girls, here is a list of our classroom rules. It will be easier for you to remember them if you can see them. I feel we all need to see rules to remember them."

Well, how did I know he meant only boys and

girls needed to see them? I'm not sure what made me do this, but the day after Mr. Blister announced the importance of seeing the classroom rules, I saw a stack of those post-it stick-on notes on his desk. I grabbed a few off his desk and wrote one class rule on each one.

"*Phoebe Flower*, what are you doing?" Mr. Blister shouted in the middle of his lesson on sinking and floating.

It got very quiet in the classroom. I was sitting in the front row, so no one knew why Mr. Blister was shouting. "Turn around, young lady, and show the class how you spend your time while I'm teaching a very important lesson!"

I turned around and at exactly the same second every boy and girl in the classroom screamed with laughter.

"Mr. Blister," I cried out, "you said it was important for everyone to see rules to remember them. I wanted to make sure you saw them, too. The rules are behind your desk so how could you see them?"

"Phoebe, take those post-it stickers off your face this instant, go to the girls' room and wash your face and then go to Dr. Nicely's office and try to explain that to her."

Dr. Nicely didn't like seeing me again. She didn't

like the reason I put the post-it stickers on my face either. She didn't even smile. She said I was being disrespectful to Mr. Blister and she was going to have to let my mother know. I begged her not to. I said I was being silly and I was so, so sorry and I would write a letter to Mr. Blister and beg him to forgive me and I would never do anything like that again. I promised, if she gave me one more chance, I would change forever. "Please, oh, please, Dr. Nicely," I begged, "my mom has been in such a good mood lately."

"Oh, Phoebe, you are lucky I like you," Dr. Nicely said, "One chance, that's it. I don't want to see you in here again, unless it's to show me something you've done well. Do you understand? I'll have to call your parents next time. I'll just have to."

"Thank you, thank you, thank you, Dr. Nicely. I'll never forget you for this. I'll even name my first child after you." I hugged her.

"Remember our deal, Phoebe," she sighed.

From that moment on, my life was going to change.

3
Father
Fix-It-Up

"Phoebe," my mom calls to me when I walk into the house, "Robbie has called the house three times in five minutes. Where have you been?"

"Oh, just outside playing hide and seek with Buddy Dog," I tell her. "What does he want?"

"I didn't ask him, but he sure seems excited about something," Mom says.

The phone rings again. "I'll get it!" I call out, "Hello. Yeah. Hi, what's up, Rob? Are you kidding me? No way! This is the greatest! I'm on my way!"

"What did he say, Phoebe?" Mom asks.

"He's got a computer," I tell her, "Do you believe it? Robbie's got a computer and he said I can come over and use it. See ya, Mom."

"Do you have homework, Phoebe?" my mom asks me.

"Just a teeny, weeny, little bit, Mom, and maybe I can do it on Robbie's computer. I promise I won't be long," I answer.

"If you go to Robbie's now, you'll have to stay in and do homework tonight, Phoebe," Mom yells after me.

Robbie's computer was more beautiful than my dad's silver and black Harley motorcycle he bought right before he and Mom got their divorce. We have computers at school, but I never used one without an adult looking over my shoulder. There were so many signs and words on the screen that I just stared and stared at it until Robbie started to shake me. "Phoebe, wake up," he says, "Don't you want to use it?"

"Sure, tell me how to start it," I say.

For two hours Robbie and I play on the computer. I write him a letter and he writes me one. We both write one to Mr. Blister. Mine says I am sorry for being disrespectful. Robbie asks him why an apple doesn't sink. You can erase anything you write by pushing a button and there's no eraser mark. We play Checkers and Concentration until his mother calls, "Robbie, time for dinner. Phoebe, do you want to eat dinner here?"

"Sure, I do, Mrs. Vaughn, but my mom's already started to make dinner for us. Thanks, though, and I'll be back. I love this computer."

"Anytime, Phoebe, anytime," Mrs. Vaughn answers.

At dinner, I tell Mom and Amanda and Walter about Robbie's computer. "It is so beautiful and you can do so many things on it. If you don't spell a word right, it fixes it for you. You don't have to use a dictionary. Robbie says that someday he'll be able to write letters to people in different countries and get one back on the same day. Can we get one, Mom?"

"Phoebe, computers cost a lot of money. We won't be able to afford one for a long time. Besides, Amanda's birthday is next week and I've been saving all my extra money to get her something special. I hope you've thought about your sister's birthday."

"Of course, I think about it almost every day, Mom," I say and smile at Amanda, "I could never forget my favorite sister's birthday. I was just asking."

"I'm your only sister, Phoebe," Amanda says, "and, if I had my way, I'd only have a brother."

"Amanda, that isn't nice," Mom squints her eyes at Amanda.

"What do you want for your birthday, Amanda?" I ask her.

"Something you can never use if I get them, that's for sure," Amanda glares at me. "I want rollerblades. You can't even walk without tripping over something, Phoebe. You could never rollerblade, that's for sure."

"That's what you know!" I tell her, "I am the fastest runner in my third grade class, Amanda. I bet I can run faster than you," I yell.

"That's great that you can run, Phoebe. You just have to learn how to walk and you'll be fine," she laughs.

"Could we have one dinner without you two fighting? Please!" Mom looks down at her plate and takes a deep breath.

After dinner my mom says, "Phoebe," as she grabs me by the arm and pulls me into the hall closet, "I have saved up enough money to buy Amanda rollerblades for her birthday. It's a secret and you can't tell her. I want to hide them so it's a big surprise. Can I put them under your bed? She'll never look there."

"Wow, you really got her rollerblades, Mom?" I ask, "Can I see them?"

"Yes, they're out in the car and I'm going to sneak them up to your room. I spent a long time thinking about where I should hide them and I decided no human would even try to enter *your* room and if they did they'd have to be an acrobat or a gorilla to get to your bed and then, if they tried to look under your bed . . . well, that's a whole other story. Sometimes I wonder what's growing under there, Phoebe."

"Mom, I just cleaned my room last week," I tell her.

"Well, anyway, Phoebe," Mom says, "You can

peek, but *don't*, and, I repeat, *don't* even think of putting them near your feet. You must have knee guards and elbow guards and a helmet before you wear them. Repeat after me, Phoebe, I will not think of putting them near my feet. "

"As Dr. Nicely says, 'You can't control your thoughts, but you can control your actions.' Don't worry, Mom, I don't want to touch those dumb things," I tell my mother. "I'm going to have a new tree house anyway. Dad is going to help me fix it up when he comes up next week. I'll be way too busy to think about silly rollerblades."

"Thank you, Phoebe. I'm going to jump in the shower, now. Will you watch Walter for me, please?" Mom asks, "I'll only be a minute."

"Sure, Mom, I love to watch Walter, but where's Amanda?" I am curious.

"She ran to the grocery store for me. We were out of milk. She should be back in a little while," Mom answers.

I want so badly to look at those rollerblades, but I promised my mom and a promise is a promise. I go play trucks with Walter, but no matter how hard I try, I can't stop thinking about them. That night I go to sleep and dream about rollerblading down the side of a mountain, doing flips and cartwheels as I rollerblade.

Dad comes on Friday night to celebrate Amanda's birthday. He is planning on being here for four days. I am so excited to see him, I greet him at the door with a huge bear hug. "Dad, you've got to come outside and look at the tree house. Robbie and I have great plans for it. I told him you'd help us."

"Easy, Phoebe, I just got here. First, I have to wish the birthday girl a happy birthday and then we'll go outside. I promise I will help you. How are you anyway? I heard about your A+ essay. Now, that's my girl!"

"I've been great, Dad! Robbie has a new computer and he lets me use it to do my homework and Mr. Blister said that was OK as long as I did the homework and not Robbie."

"Great news, Phoebe! Maybe someday I can afford to get you kids one of your own." Dad hugs me tightly.

The birthday party is really fun. Dad and Mom don't argue once. Dad doesn't get mad when Mom forgets where she hid the birthday cake. Even I think it's weird that she hid it in the dishwasher.

I don't care that Amanda gets all the attention. She loves her rollerblades even though she can't use them until Mom gets her a helmet and knee and wrist guards. I bought her some bubble bath, Walter got her an electric toothbrush and Buddydog got her some stick-on fake nails. Dad got her a pearl bracelet from some expensive store in New York City. He says she is grown up enough to wear grown-up jewelry. He also got her a guide book of Washington, DC.

"I hear my oldest daughter is going to visit the president!" Dad says with a giant grin.

"Yes, I am, Dad." Amanda brags, "Everyone knows I'll win. And . . . I also have an announcement to make."

We all stop eating our cake and wait for Amanda to speak.

"Since I am now fourteen years old, from this moment on, I want all of you to call me Mandy," Amanda announces. I will only answer to Mandy at home, at school, and with my friends."

"Mom, can Amanda do this?" I cry out.

"Can Mandy do this?" Amanda reminds me.

"I guess she can, Phoebe," Mom sighs and looks at my dad.

On Saturday, Dad keeps his promise and helps Robbie and me fix up our tree house. He builds a roof with shingles he finds in the garage and makes a rope ladder that we can use to climb up to the tree house. He tells us he has an old pair of binoculars we can use as long as we don't spy on the neighbors.

4
Broken Bones
and Dreams

When Monday morning comes around, I am nervous about the meeting Dad and Mom and I are going to have with Dr. Getset. I like being alone with Dr. Getset. My parents being there is a very different story.

"Hi, Mr. and Mrs. Flower," Dr. Getset says, "I am so glad you both could come in. Have a seat. I would also like to meet Amanda and Walter, too, and of course, Buddydog."

I can tell Mom and Dad are nervous, but they shake his hand and sit down.

"I know you are eager to get to the point of this meeting, so I will," Dr. Getset explains.

Dr. Getset is great! Both my parents laugh about

his dog, Go, and how he got the name. Then Dr. Getset tells them that the results of my tests show that I have ADD.

"What we can do for Phoebe is our main concern," Dad says.

"Well, there are several things you can do," Dr. Getset says. "Mr. Blister is already using different ideas in the classroom to help her. Right, Phoebe?"

"Yes, he is!" I smile at Dr. Getset. I think he heard about the post-it stickers.

"She can also take medication. Several children at our school take it and it helps them pay attention. Also, I know of some high school students that tutor children from our school. They do it for extra credit, so it wouldn't cost you anything. That might help Phoebe take more of an interest in her homework."

"We can do that. Is there anything else?" Mom wonders.

"Well, Mrs. Flower, you can help Phoebe get organized," Dr. Getset says.

To my surprise, Mom answers, "I've always wanted to be more organized myself, Dr. Getset, and I know this sounds crazy, but I don't know how. If I have trouble, how can I help Phoebe?"

"Well, why don't you two work on that together? I have pamphlets that suggest lots of ideas to help kids and adults. If you are more organized, Mrs. Flower, that will help Phoebe." Dr. Getset smiles when he says that, but I feel like crying. I stare my mom's face.

Dad puts his hand on Mom's arm and tells Dr. Getset that Mom is a wonderful mother.

"Oh, I'm sure she is! You can't have a terrific, loving daughter like Phoebe, if you don't have a wonderful mother. Do either of you have any questions?" Dr. Getset asks.

"How will Phoebe take this medication if she's in school?" Mom asks.

"There now are several new medications for ADD that last all day. Phoebe can take one before she comes to school. You'll have to visit your pediatrician, though, before you start the medication," Dr. Getset explains. "If you have any questions, call me day or night, here or at home. I want the very best for Phoebe, too!"

When I get home from school that day, Dad is packing to go back to NY, but he says he wants to talk to me before he leaves. He and Mom and I sit on the steps on the back porch. Dad knows this is my favorite place to sit.

"I like Dr. Getset, Phoebe, and I can tell he likes you, too," Dad smiles, "I know he wants to help you. I just want to go over what he said today so we are all on the same page."

What a Dad thing to say, I think, but I just chuckle.

"OK, first you are going to the pediatrician, right, Phoebe?"

"Righto, Dad, and there's no problemo there because I love, love, love my pediatricians," I tell him. I really do love both of them. They are the funniest doctors in the world and even when I'm getting a shot they make me laugh. Their names are Dr. Zach Black and Dr. Sue Blew.

"Before we go to the pediatrician," Mom says, "Phoebe, you and I are going to make charts to help us get organized. I have already been reading the pamphlet Dr. Getset gave me."

"And, Phoebe, your mother will be looking to find someone to help you with your homework," Dad explains. "Don't give her a hard time with this."

"Gotcha, Dad," I nod my head. No reason to upset Dad before he leaves to go back to New York.

"Mandy and Phoebe, I'm driving Dad to the train station and taking Walter with me. Can you two stay alone without fighting while I'm gone?" Mom asks us.

"Of course, Mother," Amanda answers, "I am fourteen and almost an adult."

"Phoebe?" Mom asks.

"Mother, you know me. I'm a terrific loving little girl," I tell her.

As soon as Mom and Dad leave, Amanda rushes into the house and up the stairs.

"Where are you going?" I yell after her.

"Where do you think?" Amanda yells back, "I'm going rollerblading, Phoebe, and you better not tell Mom. Do you understand?"

"Amanda, don't. If Mom finds out, she will be so mad," I tell her.

"Amanda? Amanda? Sorry, Phoebe, I don't know anyone by that name. Besides, I've wanted these for six months, Phoebe. I can't wait another day to use them. I don't care if I don't have knee and wrist guards and a helmet, yet. Those are for babies, anyway. You better keep your mouth shut, too." Amanda warns me as she sits on the front steps and puts on her rollerblades.

"I won't tell," I promise, "but don't say I didn't warn you." I don't mind being the one *not* getting in trouble for once.

I sit on the front step and watch Amanda wobble down the street. She isn't doing too badly for the first time on roller blades. She needs to stand up straighter, though. Amanda turns around and heads back to our house smiling and waving at me.

26

"Hey, Phoebe, look at m_____ ahhhhhhhhhhhh!"

Amanda must have hit a crack in the sidewalk. She flies up in the air and lands hard on her side. "OOOH, AWH!" she screams. "PHOEBE!"

I race over to where Amanda's lying. "Are you OK? " I ask.

"NO! DO I LOOK OK? My arm, Phoebe, get somebody!" Amanda starts to cry.

"Mrs. Vaughn is a nurse. I'll get her." I run toward Robbie's, but Mrs. Vaughn is already heading towards me.

"I saw Amanda fall, Phoebe. Is she OK?" Mrs. Vaughn asks me.

I almost tell Mrs. Vaughn it's "Mandy" now, but instead I say, "I don't think so. She says her arm hurts."

Mrs. Vaughn helps Amanda sit up. She takes off her rollerblades and sets them on the lawn. "I'll have to drive you to the hospital, Amanda. Your wrist is swollen."

"Mom will kill me!" Amanda cries.

Well, no such luck, Mom doesn't kill Amanda. When Mom sees how much pain Amanda is in, she doesn't say one word about her using the rollerblades without permission. If I took those rollerblades, I would be dead and buried in the back yard by now!

The doctor at the hospital explains to Amanda that she has a fractured wrist and that she'll have to stay home from school for a week and a half and wear a cast on her arm for at least six weeks. Amanda sobs.

Two days after the accident, I discover I'm the one that should have been sobbing. I have to set the table and do the dishes by myself *and* I have to help Amanda get dressed in the morning. Now that's something to cry about! It's been nothing but "poor Mandy this" and "poor Mandy that."

"Watch my arm, Phoebe! Don't be such a klutz!"

Amanda yells. "Mom, Phoebe is hurting me!"

"Phoebe, try to be gentle with poor Mandy. She is very upset. Her fractured wrist is the arm that she writes with. Now she doesn't think she will enter the contest to go to Washington. I know she's acting miserable, but you'd be upset too if you couldn't write," Mom tries to explain.

Upset! Is she kidding? What a great excuse not to have to do homework.

The next day, I overhear Mom on the phone. "Dr. Nicely, this is Mrs. Flower. My daughter, who used to be Amanda Flower and is now only answering to Mandy Flower, has had an accident. She won't be able to come to school for a week and a half. Dr. Getset mentioned having a high school girl tutor Phoebe, and I wondered if I could get the same girl to tutor Mandy and Phoebe. Do you have any twofers? Get it, Dr. Nicely, 'two for one' deals. Hee, hee."

How silly, a tutor, I thought. What can a tutor teach me that Mr. Blister can't? Just wait until she sees how smart Amanda is and how smart I'm not. I decide to keep my thoughts to myself. Mom has had one bad day after the other.

The next day after school, Mom takes me aside

and whispers that she arranged to get a tutor for Mandy and me. "Her name is Constance, Phoebe, and she is in high school and she is a very smart girl. She will be coming on Monday, Wednesday, and Friday. She's in the living room helping Mandy and when she's through it will be your turn to work with her and I don't want you to give her any trouble."

5
Love vs.
Hate

"Are you kidding me?" I yell. "You mean I have to go sit and do more school work? I honestly can't today, Mom. Robbie and I are planning to play solitaire on his computer. I promised him, and a promise is a promise. And, I'm not going to talk to any Constance from France with ants in her pants."

"That is not funny, Phoebe," Mom stares at me. "If you talk like that again, the next time you leave this house Robbie will have forgotten who you are. Constance is here for you because *you* have ants in your pants."

"Yes, and excuse us for listening, but Constance is here for me because I have the highest average in my class and I want to maintain that average," Amanda says as she enters the kitchen with Constance. "For example, solitaire comes from the word, solitary, which means alone. Robbie can play solitaire by himself. Constance, this is Phoebe. She needs a lot of help. She can't even remember her sister's name."

I really want to hate Constance, but she is beautiful and smart and she wears an ankle bracelet made from real gold. I know because I ask her. When she asks me where I want to go to do my homework I say, "My room."

"Where?" my mother asks and then looks like she might faint. But she smiles sweetly and only remarks about the "Messy Bessy" Phoebe that lives in that room.

"Cool!" says Constance when she sees the sneaker poster on my wall. "Where did you get a poster of twenty different kinds of sneakers? I like the blue high tops the best."

Constance helps me with my math problems. She teaches me to think about the problems and then asks me to draw the picture that I see in my mind. Then we do the number part. I love it when she reads the number stories to me. She reads like an actress. I can't wait for her to come again.

On Wednesday, I race off the school bus and into the house.

"Hey, Phoebe," Robbie yells from the bus, "can you come over today? I can come to your house if you want. Maybe we can play Chess in the tree house."

"Well . . . ah, I don't think so Rob, I have to check. I might have to fold some laundry for my mother. I'll call you!" I tell Robbie. Robbie is good at keeping secrets, but I want to be very careful that no one knows I am being tutored.

"So, Mom, when will Constance be finished with Amanda?" I ask when I walk in the door. "Doesn't Amanda have to go back to school soon? She probably doesn't want to miss one more second of work."

"Her name is Mandy, now. I know it's hard to change, Phoebe, but please try. The doctor said Mandy could go back after ten days," Mom explains, "She has to be very careful with her wrist, Phoebe. You do know she is *very* upset about not being able to write her essay and win the trip to Washington, don't you?"

"Yes, Mother, I am sad about that, too." I say, with my fingers crossed behind my back. I'm not sad at all. In fact, I am so, so, so happy that Amanda finally won't get something she wants. If she won that contest, I'd have to stick my face in ice water and freeze on a fake smile and pretend I think it's just absolutely wonderful that Amanda is visiting the president of the United States.

Finally, Constance comes into the kitchen. "Your turn, Phoebe Flower. What a great name you have! Do you know there's an eastern United States bird called a phoebe. It's brownish gray and light yellow." Constance smiles at me. "What kind of homework do you have today, Phoebe?"

"I have to write an essay on something I want to know about," I tell her.

"And what could that be?" Amanda asks.

"I want to know if all animals have belly buttons."

"Very, very cool!" Constance says, "Let's find out!"

Amanda rolls her eyes. "A bird name does fit you nicely, Phoebe."

When we get to my room, I ask Constance if she has a sister.

"Yes, I do," she says. "I have a sister and a brother, just like you, Phoebe. In fact, my sister and I remind me of you and Mandy."

"That's too bad," I tell her.

"Not really," Constance says, "I can tell you two

feel about each other just as my sister and I felt about each other."

"So your older sister hated you. Is that what you're saying? And, you could never figure out why. When you were little she liked you, and read stories to you and let you sit on her lap, but when you got older she thought you were like dog biscuit gravy."

"Well, it was something like that, Phoebe, except that I was the older sister and for a long time I hated my younger sister."

"What happened?"

"Well, I finally figured out that I didn't hate her, I was just jealous of her and wished I could be like she was," Constance says.

"Well, there is no way on this planet that Amanda would wish she could be like me."

"I think you're wrong, Phoebe." Constance moves closer to me. "You are everything Mandy wishes she could be. You aren't worried about good grades. You are smart in ways she can't be and you are clever and happy all the time, even when you are in trouble. You are not afraid of anything, Phoebe. Mandy probably wants to be like you are."

"Constance, Amanda would never want to be like me. I get sent to the principal's office so much that I can tell you if Dr. Nicely flosses her teeth in the morning or at night, and that's not because we're friends," I tell Constance.

"I forgot to say funny, Phoebe. You are very funny," Constance laughs.

The next day Mom picks me up early from school, so I can go to the pediatrician. I laugh out loud when I see the sign in front of their office, even though I've seen it a zillion times. It says:

| Doctors |
| Black and Blew |
| *happily* |
| take care of any boo boo. |

"Hi, Phoebe, what brings you here today?" Dr. Blew asks me, as she grabs my chart and walks over to the table where I'm sitting.

My mom begins to explain what Dr. Getset told us about ADD.

"Well, Phoebe, I agree with Dr. Getset," Dr. Blew says. She takes her pointer finger and touches my forehead. "Remember that time you decided to ride your tricycle down the front porch stairs because you thought it would be faster than walking?"

"Well, sort of," I say, "I remember the blood, mostly."

"Yes, well that's what this scar is from," Dr. Blew continues to talk as she moves her finger to the scar on my knee, "Remember the time you jumped off the Merry-Go-Round before it stopped?"

"Well, I didn't think I'd get hurt from that," I shrug.

"That's why I had to put stitches right there," Dr. Blew hugs me. "Yes, Phoebe, I have seen you in here many, many times since you were a baby. You are one of my favorite patients, of course, and I love to see you, but you are usually getting hurt because you're not thinking about getting hurt. Trying the medication that Dr. Getset recommends is a good idea. Mrs. Flower, please call me in three or four days and let me know how Phoebe's doing. And Phoebe . . . please wait until the Merry-Go-Round stops."

The next time Constance comes, we skip backwards to the library together to find information for my paper. She says she has never done that before and she laughs all the way there. When we get back home, we go to my room. I open the door for her, do a spin around, and say, "Voila, Constance, do you notice anything different about my room?"

"Different?" she says, "Phoebe, it looks like an enormous brontosaurus visited your bedroom and sneezed all your stuff out the window. Where did it all go?"

"So you like it, huh?" I ask her feeling very proud of myself. "Well, I just got tired of the same joke."

"What's that?" Constance asks me.

"Mom would ask me to pick up my room and I'd say, 'I can't, it's too heavy'."

Constance laughs outloud. Then, she shows me how to draw some animals for my project. We work for about an hour without getting up even once. My mother asks if Constance wants to stay for dinner.

"Dinner! I just got home from school, Mom," I say.

"Time flies when you're drawing belly buttons," Mom laughs.

"Don't tell me that Constance is wasting her time showing Phoebe how to draw a belly button, Mom," I hear Amanda whisper to my mother.

The next morning, I can't wait to go to school and read my belly button story. I hop out of bed, jump down the stairs two at a time, eat my cereal in three bites, take my pill, and check my chart. I check off "make bed" and "flush toilet." Oh, rats, I didn't brush my teeth. I run back upstairs, brush my teeth and come down and check it off. I notice Mom has only two things checked off on her chart this morning. *Yeah, Phoebe!*

I'm on the corner before Robbie gets there.

"Wait a minute, Phoebe, what's up with you?"

"I'm up, Robbie, and ready to go to school and read my homework."

"Who are you and where's the Phoebe Flower

who used to live in that blue house over there? The Phoebe Flower who thought her dog was a wizard, and everyday that Phoebe Flower would walk by her dog and say, 'Please, please, please, Buddy-wizard-dog, wag your tail, use your magic powers, turn me into a dog and I will be your loyal pooch friend for the rest of my life. Please Buddy-wizard-dog stop me from getting on that school bus'."
Robbie falls to his knees and clasps his hands together.

"OK, Rob, you're right, I've changed. I realized Buddydog couldn't turn me into a dog, so I stopped asking him. But, he is the smartest dog I've ever known," I laugh.

"Phoebe, that's not what's changed. You've changed. You act like you want to go to school," Robbie yells at me.

"I thought that was the idea, Robbie. I thought everyone wanted me to want to go to school." I am feeling confused.

I think about what Robbie says all day. I can't believe I'm liking school. Do I really like school? I don't seem to mind it anymore. It feels good when Mr. Blister says, "Phoebe, I love seeing your home-work on my desk." Then he marks it and I get most of it right. It feels good to feel smart.

On the bus ride home from school, I ask,

"Robbie, do you want to play cards in the tree house after dinner?"

Robbie's so happy that I ask him, he pulls a pack of cards out of his back pocket and says, "Ready when you are, Phoebe! Come on over and do your homework on my computer after school, so your mom will let you go to the tree house after dinner."

Robbie must be missing me.

6
A New View

That night after dinner, we grab flashlights, binoculars, and a brown bag of peanut butter sandwiches and pretzels. Robbie fills up old water bottles with Kool-Aid. I grab a bag of M&M's that I had hidden under the couch. We climb up the rope ladder my dad made for us. It's as quiet as a falling snowflake when we get up there. We both close our eyes and count to three. Robbie guesses first. "I can hear the train. I think it's passing the mall. Can you hear it, Phoebe?"

"Yep, I do, and I hear Mrs. Burns washing her dishes. Can you hear her, Rob?"

"I think I can hear Prissy Fasola playing the piano. Do you?" Rob asks me.

"Yeah, but I also hear some weird whining sound. What do you think that is?" I ask him. "It sounds like a cat."

"Beats me, Phoebe. Maybe it is a cat. It could be a baby crying."

"No, I don't think it's a baby," I say. "Hand me the binoculars. Let me look."

"Oh wow, oh wow, oooh wow, Robbie! That's it!" I scream at him.

"What's it, Phoebe? Stop yelling. The world will know we're up here," Robbie warns me.

"This is why I'm liking school. I just figured it out," I whisper.

"OK, I give up. Why do you, now, like school, Phoebe?" Robbie asks me.

"Look out there into the back yard and tell me what you see," I say to him.

"I see lots of tree shadows and light from your house and a little sliver of the moon and a cat hopping over our fence and your car parked in your driveway and Walter's tricycle tipped over by the garbage can. That's about it. Why? What are you saying?" Robbie wonders.

"Exactly! I knew you'd say that. Now look through these binoculars and tell me what you see." I tell him.

"I can see into my house and my mom is eating dessert. She's supposed to be on a diet. Shame,

shame on her! If I look closer I can tell exactly what she's eating. Munchy Crunchy chocolate ice cream, that's *my* favorite! But, what's your point, Phoebe?"

"My point is . . . looking through the binoculars is sort of like why I am starting to like school, Robbie. When you are wearing the binoculars you only see one thing, but one thing closely. Now, when I'm in school I don't see everything around me like I did. It's like my eyes have become binoculars and I see one thing and I want to learn about it. Everything about school seemed so hard before. Now it seems to make sense to me. I know why I'm learning stuff and I want to learn it. I read and I hardly ever daydream anymore." I grab the binoculars away from Robbie and put them to my eyes. "For example, now I see . . . now I see . . . "

"What? Come on Phoebe, what? What do you see?"

"Robbie, shh, look through these into Amanda's room," I tell him.

"Are you nuts, Phoebe? I'd rather spy on the president of the United States than your sister. She'll kill us if she sees us. Besides you promised your dad you wouldn't spy on anyone."

"She isn't going to see us, Robbie. Just take a look." I hand Robbie the binoculars. "Amanda's the cat, Rob."

"Wow, Phoebe, She's going crazy. She's

throwing papers all around her room. What's the matter with her?" Robbie asks me.

"The whole matter with Amanda began on the day she was born. I don't think we have enough time to talk about that now, but I will tell you what's the matter with her tonight. Amanda was planning to win the *What Makes a Good Citizen* writing contest and go visit the president of the United States and eat lobster. The contest is judged not only by what is said in the essay, but how neat it is. Amanda fractured her wrist, so she can't write and now she won't win. I'm glad because I won't have to hear about how smart she is and Amanda is very sad. Boo, hoo!"

"Why doesn't she just type it?" Robbie asks.

"Because, Robbie," I begin to explain, "Amanda never learned how to type because her hand writing is so perfect it looks like it is typed. Every letter is just flawless. That's why all my teachers would say, "Oh, you can't be Amanda Flower's sister. She writes flawlessly. Why don't you try to write like Amanda, Phoebe? Then we'd be able to read what you write. Well, I did try and I couldn't and I guess it's too bad for Amanda, isn't it? That's why I am so glad you let me use your computer, Robbie."

"Are you just going to let her cry like that, Phoebe?" Robbie asks me.

"No, actually, Robbie, I was planning on calling

the White House tomorrow morning and saying, 'Mr. Pres., my sister has a boo boo on her hand and can't come and eat lobster with you. I hope you won't be too disappointed'." I laugh so hard I almost fall out of the tree.

"Phoebe, I never knew you were so mean." Robbie shakes his head.

"*Mean*! *Mean*! How can you call me mean, Robert Vaughn III? I am nice. Amanda is mean. She has been mean to me all my life. She hates me. I don't hate her. I'm just so glad I don't have to hear her brag to me one more time about how perfect she is."

"Well, if that's true, Missy Nice Sister," Robbie stares at me, "then why don't you do something nice for her. First of all, try calling her by her new name."

For twenty minutes I sit and say nothing. Robbie says nothing either.

"What exactly is it that you think I can do to help *Amandy*, Robert?" I quietly ask.

Robbie shrugs his shoulders.

"Come on, Robbie, I know you are thinking something."

Robbie just sits and stares at Amanda sobbing on her bed.

"OK, you are going to have to help me, Robbie, and you and I could both get in a lot of trouble doing this, y'know." I remind him.

Robbie and I begin to make a plan. We decide that I'm going to pretend to go upstairs to bed. I wait for Walter, Mom and Amanda to go to bed; then I sneak into Amanda's room, find her essay, and signal Robbie by blinking my bedroom light three times to let him know I got it. Then, I tiptoe from my house to Robbie's house, where he will meet me at his back door. Then the two of us will take turns typing out a nice neat version of Amanda's essay, *What Makes A Good Citizen,* on Robbie's computer.

We climb down the ladder laughing and singing as loudly as we can.

"Phoebe, shhh!" my mother says as she opens the back door to our house. "Be quiet. You should be in the house getting ready for bed."

"As a matter of fact, I was just about to do that. Right, Rob?" I say and wink.

"Yes, me too, Mrs. Flower, I'm off to dreamland," Robbie says. "You should go to bed early tonight, too. You look very tired."

"Is that so, Robbie? Well, for your information I *am* tired, but I think I look pretty good tonight."

"Oh, you always look good, Mrs. Flower. Tired sometimes means good," Robbie says.

"That's enough, Rob," I whisper to him. "You're overdoing it."

"Well, good night, Mom," I say, and give her a big kiss.

"You're going to bed this early?" Mom asks. "Do you feel OK?"

"Yes, fine, Mom, I just got tired climbing up and down the ladder of our tree house," I explain, "Is Amandamandy around?"

"Tomorrow's the day her essay is due. I think she gave up trying to write it. She is so upset. I wish I could think of a way to help her. Maybe I'll go check on her."

"No, no, no, Mom, I'll check on her. I'll tell her some jokes to cheer her up."

"That's sweet, Phoebe, but Mandy has never liked your jokes. Maybe you shouldn't do that tonight," Mom warns me.

"Good idea, I'll just say good night to her. You relax, Mom. I'll take care of everything. By the way, is Walter asleep yet?"

"Sound asleep, Phoebe, so tiptoe upstairs, please, and thanks for being so kind to Amanda. I know she doesn't always appreciate you."

"That's the truest thing you've ever said." I hug my mom.

So far the plan is working better than any FBI agent could have planned. I open Amanda's door slowly and peek into her room. She has fallen asleep

49

on top of her bed with her clothes on. Her essay is torn and thrown all over the floor. What a mess! How am I going to get all of it? I decide to pick it up now, while she is breathing heavily. I crawl into her room on my stomach and start to pick up the paper scraps one at a time. I finally have almost every single piece tucked into my tee shirt. Just as I start to crawl backwards out the door my foot hits Amanda's waste basket and knocks it over. Oh, no!

"PHOEBE!!!" Amanda screams, "What are you doing here? I told you never to come in here and I mean it. Now, get out!"

"Amanda, my bouncy ball accidentally rolled across the hall into your room," I lie to her, "I had to find it. I'll never come in again. I promise. Now, go back to sleep."

"My name is *Mandy* and you are such a baby, Phoebe. When are you going to stop playing with balls and grow up! Get out NOW!!" Amanda was yelling very loudly.

"Phoebe, what's going on?" my mom calls up the stairs.

"I didn't tell her a joke, Mom, I swear I didn't," I say. "I'm going to bed now, for sure."

"Good, and good night, Phoebe," Mom says, "I love you!"

7
Lost but
Found

The first part of the plan isn't going quite as perfectly as we planned. I have to grab my right hand tightly with my left hand, so it doesn't take that torn up essay I have in my shirt and throw it in the basket. Amanda is so mean to me. How could Robbie have called me mean? I'm the nice sister. Why am I doing this for her, anyway?

Robbie is waiting, so I better keep going with the plan. All I need now is for my mother to go to sleep. I wait in my room for what seems like an hour. I sneak down the stairs like an old cat and peek over the railing. My mother is pretending to watch television in her favorite blue chair while she snores. Should I wake her up or just go for it?

I slither out the door without one single sound. I know, if I wanted to, I could make a great criminal. Robbie is waiting at his back door with his pointer finger at his lip. "Shh, Phoebe, everyone just went to bed. What took you so long? I thought you were going to flash your lights when you got the essay."

"Well, Robbie, after Amanda called me a baby and screamed at me never to enter her precious room again for the rest of my life, I took a trip to the bathroom and stared down at the toilet thinking how much easier it would be to flush this essay than to try to tape it together and type it for her," I tell him.

"Well, then, why didn't you?" Robbie asks me.

"I don't know. I guess I like being called, Missy Nice Sister," I laugh.

"Let's get to work, Missy," Robbie says.

It takes us a long time to tape the paper pieces together. We're missing about five small pieces. Good thing Robbie knows how to be a good citizen. He has soda and potato chips for us when we take a break. We take turns using the computer. It checks the spelling and says where to put the periods and question marks. When we finish, it's almost midnight, but neither one of us is tired.

"Phoebe, I've never seen you sit still so long or work so much without getting up to do something dumb like peel a banana or clean out the pencil sharpener," says Robbie.

"Enough about me, Rob. You are doing a great job, too." I am feeling pretty good about how I can help Amanda. " I told you, Rob, this kind of thing is easier now. I think Dr. Getset knew what he was talking about. I am smart. I just needed to concentrate better."

"OK, now the final stage of the plan, Phoebe. Are you ready?" Robbie asks me.

"Ready as Cinderella was to find her prince," I say.

"Don't forget to signal me when you get to your room," Robbie warns me. "One flash if everything is fine. Two flashes if everything's not fine. Three flashes if you're caught sneaking in."

"I think two and three are the same, Robbie," I remind him.

"Well, don't forget, Phoebe, and good luck." Robbie shakes my hand.

I skip over to my back door and see that there's good news and better news. The first good news is that my mother has gone to bed. The better news is that she forgot to lock the door before she went to bed. She always forgets to lock it, but lately she's been trying very hard to remember to do what's on her chart. I hope she didn't check it off if she didn't do it.

I have a five page paper in my hand that has to get to Amanda's room tonight without one wrinkle in it. Soon, this paper will be in the hands of the president of the United States. I feel just like I did the day in gym I jumped rope two hundred and sixteen times and won the jump rope contest; except this time . . . I used my brain. I sit down on the back steps and take a deep breath.

When I get upstairs, I slide the essay under Amanda's door. I almost forget to signal Robbie that all is fine. I know he is probably waiting. I flash the lights once, then I fall into bed.

The next morning, I hear Mom calling my name to wake me up. I'm dreaming I'm in a jail cell, trying to escape with a peanut butter sandwich in my mouth. If I drop the sandwich I won't get anything else to eat for the rest of my life.

"Mandy, Phoebe, what's going on up there?" Mom yells.

I flop down the stairs and sit staring at my cereal bowl.

"Phoebe, eat!" my mom says.

"Where's Amanda?" I ask my mom.

"Very good question. She'd better hurry because her bus is coming. I think she is just moving slowly because she's sad, very sad," Mom says.

Amanda bursts into the room with, "Good morning, Mother, Phoebe and Walter!" She even pats Buddydog on the head. "I love you, Mom. You're the best mother in the whole wide world. Amanda kisses Mom on the cheek, hugs her and runs out the door with her essay in her hand singing, "Oh, What a Beautiful Morning!"

My mom sits down at the kitchen table. "OK, Phoebe, what's up?"

"I don't know what you mean," I answer my mother.

"Why is Mandy so happy today?"

"I didn't notice. Was she?" I reply.

"You know and I know and Walter knows and Buddydog knows that Amanda, Mandy, whoever she may be, is never, ever happy in the morning. Added to that is the fact that she is sure she's not going to win something. I was expecting to see orange and red flames jumping out of her mouth this morning, so don't try to fool me, Phoebe. I know you know something. I don't want to have to call Robbie and ask him. You tell me what you know."

I have no choice. I know Robbie would tell my mom the whole story, so I confess. My mom has tears in her eyes. Then she hugs me.

I hurry off to school, but all day I think about Amanda winning the essay contest.

After school, Robbie and I jump off the school bus and together we barge in the front door of my house. My mother is standing by the window holding Walter in her arms.

"Where's Amanda?" I ask.

"She's not home yet. I knew she was going to be late today because the judges were going to announce the winners after school," Mom explains to me. "I am very nervous. Let's all sit down and wait."

"Sit? I can't sit, Mom," I tell her.

All four of us start to pace. Even Walter walks around the living room in circles.

When we finally hear Amanda's footsteps walking up the front walk, the four of us jump on the couch and sit perfectly still waiting for the door to open. Amanda walks in and goes past us up the stairs and straight to her room. She closes the door.

We don't move. We wait.

Fifteen minutes pass and finally Amanda's bedroom door creaks open. She walks down the stairs and travels slowly over to the couch. She is biting the inside of her cheek.

"I'm sure you are all wondering what happened in school today." Amanda takes a deep breath. "Well, sad but true, I lost the essay contest." There was not a sound in the room. "But," she continues, "I also found out something, something very special. I found I'm not the only smart sister in this family. Phoebe, I think you're a little too big to sit on my lap, but do you want to come to my room and sit next to me on my bed? We can sing songs and read books together."

My mouth drops open. Without answering Amanda, I get up and move slowly toward her.

Amanda smiles at Mom and Walter and Robbie. "I bet you want to know how I figured out it was

Phoebe who wrote my essay, don't you?"

They all nod.

"When the judges read, 'Amanda Flower, first runner up', I thought to myself, *no one calls me Amanda, anymore, except my sister.*"

Amanda takes my hand and whispers in my ear, "Phoebe, can you teach me to skip backwards?" We walk together into her room.